No Biting Little Monster!

By Jetty & B

To my little monsters J&B

In a magical forest, there once lived a little monster named Zig. Zig was a friendly monster who loved to play with his forest friends.

But Zig had a bad habit of biting others when he got too excited.

One day, Zig was playing with his friend,
a cute bunny named Boo.

They were having
so much fun, playing catch with each other
in the forest

But suddenly, Zig got too excited and bit
Boo on the ear!

Boo was hurt and started
to cry. Zig felt terrible and didn't
know what to do.

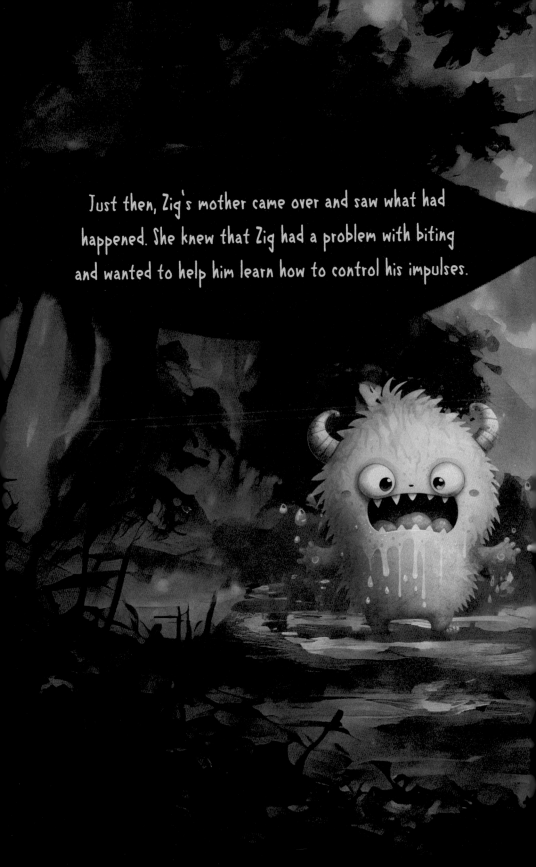

Just then, Zig's mother came over and saw what had happened. She knew that Zig had a problem with biting and wanted to help him learn how to control his impulses.

"Zig," she said, "biting is not nice. You hurt your friend, Boo.
We need to find a way for you to play without biting."

His mother took him to see the wise old owl, who was known for giving good advice to all the creatures in the forest.

The wise old owl listened to Zig's problem and thought for a moment. Then he said, "Zig, when you feel like biting, take a deep breath and count to three. This will help you calm down and think before you act."

Zig tried the owl's advice the next time he was
playing with his friends. He felt like biting again,
but he remembered to take a deep breath and count to three.

He realized that he didn't have to bite to have fun.
And he could play games with his
friends without biting.

Soon, all of Zig's friends noticed that he wasn't biting anymore. They were happy to play with him without worrying about getting hurt.

Zig and his friends continued to have fun together, playing and exploring the magical forest. And Zig knew that he had learned an important lesson about being kind and respectful to others.

5 Tips for Parents

1. **Identify Triggers:** Observe when the child is more likely to bite and try to identify triggers. It could be hunger, tiredness, overstimulation, or frustration. Addressing these triggers can help prevent biting incidents.

2. **Patience:** Be patient and understanding. Biting is a common behavior in young children and it may take time and effort to address it. Keep trying different strategies until you find what works best for the child.

3. **Teach Communication:** Help the child develop better communication skills so they can express their feelings or needs without biting. Encourage them to use words, gestures, or pictures to express themselves.

4. **Encourage Empathy:** Help the child develop empathy by talking about feelings and emotions, reading books about feelings, and encouraging them to put themselves in other people's shoes.

5. .**Seek Professional Help:** If the biting behavior persists or is severe, seek professional help from a pediatrician, child psychologist, or behavioral therapist.

Made in the USA
Monee, IL
18 December 2023